Okay, so let me just get a few things straight. I'm not kidding around, here. All of this REALLY HAPPENED. I'm not the kind of person who makes things up. Well, okay, sometimes I do . . . maybe I like stories better than I like so-called Real Life . . . but believe me, everything you're about to read is the Truth, the Whole Truth and Nothing But The Truth so help me Herbert. I didn't change anything or try to jazz it up after the fact. This is EXACTLY the way it all went down.

Well, kinda/sorta/almost.

Y'see, some of the times this is gonna look like just what it is: my ~~diary memoirs~~ ~~journal~~ diary. But other times, well . . . things are gonna get a little strange. Correction: things are gonna get a LOT strange. Like with the pictures. I'm not talking about the old photos I've taped into the book . . . y'know, the ones of me with my brother or mother or Gramma Esther. I'm talking about those OTHER pictures, THE ONES NOBODY EVER TOOK. THE ONES THAT JUST APPEARED THERE LIKE MAGIC.

You think THAT'S strange? Wait.

You're gonna see—REALLY SEE—a lot of the things that happened to me. Kind of like watching a TV show or a movie of my life jumping across the pages. And not JUST the stuff that happened to me. Every once in a while you're gonna see stuff that happened when I WASN'T EVEN AROUND.

Right. So if you don't think I'm a complete liar (which I'm not but I wouldn't blame you for thinking that I was) you've gotta ask: How could something like this happen? Ready for an answer that's gonna blow the top of your head off? Okay . . . MY DIARY'S BEEN ENCHANTED.

Yes, I said enchanted and no, I'm not kidding.

If you wanna know HOW it got enchanted, I promise I'll explain everything later. (And if you can't wait, TOO BAD: I mean, c'mon, what's a good story without a little suspense?) But I can't DO that until I explain all the OTHER weirdoramic things that have happened to me.

So here it is. My enchanted ~~memoirs diary journal~~ diary. I was thinking about giving it a Big Dramatic Title like THE BIZARRE ADVENTURES OF KATE JAMESON, FOURTEEN-YEAR-OLD MALCONTENT. But I figure there's only one title that could ever really work:

ABADAZAD

Take it or leave it. Kate

Little Martha

IN

ABADAZAD

BY FRANKLIN O. DAVIES

ILLUSTRATED BY ARTHUR N. PIERSON

for Queen Ija and those simpletons in Inconceivable—but they have no place in my city."

"You are a very bad man!" Little Martha exclaimed.

"Indeed, I am," sneered the Lanky Man, incredibly pleased with himself. "There is no more sinister specimen in all of Abadazad." With that he turned the key, locking Little Martha in the cell, then turned away and skittered down the dark corridor.

Martha had no idea what to do next. "Think, Martha, think!" she said aloud; but, for all her efforts, no useful thoughts emerged. She was seriously considering weeping for a minute or two (or three, at best), when she heard a familiar voice, echoing from across the dungeon:

"Martha?" called the voice. "Martha, is that you?"

"Professor Headstrong!" Martha squealed excitedly, knowing that if her dear friend was near she would soon be free. "Professor Headstrong, I'm over here! Quickly, quickly," she urged. "Let me out!"

"That, I'm afraid," sighed the sonorous voice, "is something I cannot do. For you see, my beloved child, I

Guess that's what the Divorce Wars do to kids. You either sink alone or swim together.

Dad ditched us when Matt was two and I was five. The Great Herbert Jameson left Brooklyn for Seattle or Portland or some stupid place—and we haven't seen him since.

Not that I really care. I mean, if the guy can't even take a minute once a year to send a birthday card, he's not worth caring about.

Anyway, with Herbert gone, Frantic Frances . . . that's my mom . . . got totally weird. She kept changing jobs (and always getting fired), taking night classes (which she never finished), going out on dates (with guys she couldn't stand)—and generally acting crazy.

I don't mean CRAZY crazy. It's not like

she thought she was getting secret messages from Martians or anything . . . but she was doing stuff like locking herself in the bathroom in the middle of the night—I guess because she didn't want to wake us up—and then crying so loud that she always did.

Or she'd show up at school sometimes . . . right in the middle of the day . . . take us out of class, and drag us home without telling us why.

We always imagined some Great Disaster: the apartment building burned to the ground, or everything we owned turned to black ash. But as soon as we'd get back—no flames in sight—Mom would walk straight into her bedroom, lock the door, and go to sleep, leaving Matty and me sitting there wondering what the heck that was all about.

Look, I understand. Sort of. I mean, your husband dumps you and leaves you alone to take care of two bratty kids. (Well, one bratty kid and a pint-sized saint.) How much fun is that?

Of course Mom wasn't exactly wrapped too tight before Herbert the Great skipped out. (I didn't start calling her Frantic Frances for nothing.) But I have to admit she did one thing right: SHE GAVE ME MATT.

First time I saw my little brother in the hospital I was crazy about him. I guess I'd been waiting my whole life for him to be born, only I didn't know it. Mom put that prune-faced squirt in my arms and it was like meeting my oldest, dearest friend . . . for the very first time. I know that doesn't make much sense, but that's how it was.

Okay, it's true that sometimes I used to call him Saint Matt the Perfect . . . but he knew I didn't mean it in a nasty way. (Well, maybe once in a while I did, but I

always felt rotten afterwards.)
And the fact is he WAS perfect, mostly.

Sure Matt got scared easy. And he kept wetting the bed till he was five. And Mr. Webster, our assistant principal, said he depended on me too

much . . . which he probably did. But so what? I depended on him, too.

He was nothing like me: never messed up in school. Never made Frantic Frances mad. He was way smart. And he was polite to everybody, even people who didn't deserve it. I bet if Dear Old Dad had come waltzing back in the house Matt wouldn't have asked him why he left or how come he never called or wrote. He just would have given Herbert a big hug and said, "Welcome home."

The truth is Matt was so young when Mom and Dad split up that he didn't really remember Herbert all that well (lucky kid), and so he could pretty much create his own version in his mind.

HIS Herbert could be anything that Matty wanted: a secret agent called away on a government mission. An alien who had to return to his home planet. Once Matt tried to convince me that Herbert was actually Merlin—y'know, the wizard from the King Arthur stories?—and he was living in an abandoned subway tunnel protecting the city from the Forces of Evil. Stupid, huh?

Wanna know what's even stupider? It was kind of fun—once in a while, anyway—to think of Herbert that way instead of the way he REALLY was: the Biggest Jerk in the History of Jerkdom.

Sometimes I think Matt made up those stories more for me than for himself. He was that kind of kid.

Anyway, the two of us shared a room and we'd stay up late a lot, just lying there in the dark—Matty in his bed, me in mine, talkingtalkingtalking. About whatever came into our heads. There was nothing I couldn't say to Matt, nothing I was afraid to share with him. And . . . I know this sounds dumb, him being so young and all . . . but he always had something to say that helped me, made me feel better.

Saint Matt had this way of looking at the world. Like he was seeing something I couldn't. That nobody else could. Like there was a whole other universe hidden underneath this one.

I dunno. I can't really explain it—but I could feel it With Matty, life was good just the way it was. Know what I mean? No? Then how about this: HE WAS MY BROTHER. And either you get that or you don't.

One of the things Matt loved more than almost anything—sometimes I think he even loved it more than me or Frances—was Abadazad.

You've heard of Abadazad, right? I mean . . . duh . . . who hasn't? Even if you're, like, illiterate and haven't read the books, you've seen the movies or cartoons . . . the toys and video games. But just in case you're totally clueless:

The first book, *Little Martha in Abadazad*, was written in 1898 by this guy named Franklin O. Davies. It was about an orphan girl who finds a magical Blue Globe that transports her to a fairyland called (what else?) Abadazad.

Sounds familiar, right? Down the rabbit hole, over the rainbow, through the wardrobe? But Abadazad did it better than all of them.

Davies wrote, I dunno, nineteen or twenty Abadazad books that were all published between 1898 and 1924, starting with *Little Martha*, then *Queen Ija of Abadazad*, *The Eight Oceans of Abadazad*, *Professor Headstrong of*

Abadazad, The Enchanted Gardens of Abadazad, The Balloonicorn in Abadazad, The Edges of Abadazad, The—

Well, I think you get the idea. After Franklin O. died, his daughter, P.J. Davies, wrote fifteen more. There are still people writing Abadazad stories today. (I only know this stuff 'cause Matt had a book called *Franklin O. Davies, Dreamer of Abadazad* that he used to make me read to him over and over. So don't think I'm some kind of nerd like those morons that go to Abadazad conventions dressed up like the Waterlogged Warlock, okay?)

I don't know how many hours Matty and I spent locked away in our bedroom, reading about Little Martha's adventures. We believed, both of us, in the REALITY of that world. We knew, with all our hearts, that every word was true.

My brother's favorite character wasn't one of the mega-popular ones like the Historceress or Mary Annette or the Burping Dragon. (I ADORED the Burping Dragon—when I was little, I mean. I had a stuffed B.D. that I slept with and dragged

Queen Ija

around with me till it completely fell apart.)
Don't get me wrong. Matty loved them. He
loved them all. But he always went for the
underdog—so of course he got himself stuck
on a second-string character, a little boy called
Master Wix.

Master Wix wasn't. A boy, that is. He was
actually an enchanted mass of wax . . . more of
a candle than a human being. But Wix believed,
with all his heart, that he was real—and Matty
believed, with all his heart, in Master Wix.

I guess that's the way it was with Franklin
O. Davies and Abadazad. He believed. None
of the books anyone else did could compare
with his. Davies wrote about Abadazad like he'd
been there. Like he knew every corner of that
place. Like he'd walked up the Living Staircase
to the capital city of Inconceivable and straight
into Queen Ija's Royal—

Hey, look, I'm fourteen now and I wouldn't
read a stupid kiddie book if you paid me. I'm
just telling you about Abadazad because it
meant so much to Matt, okay?

Anyway, I don't know why I'm going on
and on about this when what you really want
to know about is what happened that day at
The Street Fair.

The fair showed up every August. They'd block off a humongous section of Seventh Avenue and I swear you'd forget you were even in Brooklyn.

I was nine that summer, so I still (kinda/sorta) enjoyed it. Matty was six. He'd been to the fair before, but I think he was too young to really get it. That year he got it . . . and then some. It was, "Katie, look at this!" and "Katie, come over here!" I tried to make him slow down, to stay close to me, but he kept running away.

And I guess I got mad. Not MAD mad, WORRIED mad. ~~I knew that if anything happened to Matt, I could never~~

Anyway, I chased after Matty and grabbed him by the arm (not too hard, but hard enough for me to feel like a rat the second I did it).

"Hey," I said (well, maybe I yelled), "don't run away from me like that, okay? Never. Don't you know the whole city's filled with weird people who just can't wait to do weird things to little kids?"

Well, one look at the little dummy (I don't mean STUPID dumb . . . I mean dumb about the WORLD dumb) and it was clear that stuff like that had never even crossed his mind.

That's the problem with being a saint, I guess. You think everybody's Pure and Perfect like you.

Maybe I shouldn't have said anything to him . . . I mean, he was only six . . . but I guess I thought it was time he started learning what a crummy place the world can be. I wasn't trying to scare him, I was just trying to protect him. ~~Yeah, great job I did with~~ If I could do it over again, I'd shut my big stupid mouth, but that day I just kept going—

"While you're sleeping," I said, "I'M watching the ten o'clock news. You wouldn't believe some of the stuff I've seen. So stay close, okay? OKAY?"

I'm waiting for him to go white or start crying, but all he said was: "Okay . . . but I'm not worried, Katie. Long as you're around, nothing bad's ever gonna happen to me."

It was weird: All of a sudden I was the one who felt like crying. I mean, the little dummy trusted me so much. ~~And there was no way I was ever gonna let him down.~~ "C'mon," I said, taking his hand, "let's go have some fun."

Mom gave us ten dollars each that morning (she was working Saturdays at Video Magic then), and so we rode every

ride and played every game and stuffed our faces with so much junk food that we nearly barfed in stereo.

It was really a fantastic day. Too bad it didn't end there.

I was beyond pooped. Matt, on the other hand, was in sugar-overdose hyperdrive. All I wanted to do was get home, crash out on the couch and watch endless hours of dumb TV—but the kid just wouldn't let up on me: "One more ride on the boats, Katie! Just one more!"

"Look, Matt," I said, "you've been on the boats three times already and it's after six. Mom's probably home by now and you know how she gets when we're late. Five minutes past curfew and she'll be calling the cops."

But "Sinbad's Voyage" was Matty's favorite and he kept asking and asking and asking.

I had a choice: I could either get mad at him or give in. Thing is, I never could stay mad at Matty for very long, so, really, what was the point in even bothering? I rolled my eyes—the way Frantic Frances does when she just doesn't have the strength to argue anymore—and dug around in my pocket. I couldn't find anything in there but lint. "Sorry, kiddo," I said. "Outta tickets. Outta money." That's when Mr. Balloon showed up.

That was the name on the booth he came out of—"Mr. Balloon!" spelled out in big fat rainbow letters—so I guess it was his name, too. It was weird because I swear I hadn't even seen that booth till he started talking to us . . . and we'd been walking past that spot all day. Maybe it's because I always hated those guys. You've seen 'em, right? They blow up a couple of balloons and then twist them around into shapes that are supposed to look like giraffes or horses but, really, they look like creepy little monsters that crawled out from under your bed or the back of the closet. I used to have nightmares about those things when I was a kid. Even the stupid Balloonicorn in the Abadazad books used to scare me.

Anyway, we looked up . . . and up and up. He must have been, I dunno, seven feet tall. And skinny. Like he was made out of pipe cleaners instead of flesh and blood. He was wearing this clown makeup that was smeared all over his face like he didn't care how he looked . . . and he had a balloon nose that stuck out ten or fifteen feet. (Okay, so it didn't really. And he probably wasn't half as tall or skinny or spooky. Maybe I've just made him that way in my mind. Y'know, because of What Happened.)

So Mr. Balloon says to us, "If the little boy wants to go on the boat ride one more time . . . well, then, by all means, he should." He reached into his jacket and pulled out two tickets. "Exactly what's required. A short journey across the ocean and home you'll go."

I wasn't gonna take the tickets. I swear I wasn't. I mean I've heard the whole routine about not letting strangers give you stuff and blahblahblah . . . but, really, it wasn't like he was offering us a ride in his car.

And, besides, Matty gave me The Lip. Every kid knows that one. You push out your lower lip and then you get this look in your eyes like some pathetic lost puppy that's being sent to the pound. When I was a little squirt, I used to do it whenever I was totally desperate to get my greedy little hands on some new toy or whatever. Frances never bought it, but Herbert fell for it every time. You'd think because I used to pull that routine myself I'd be immune to The Lip. But one look at Matty and I totally folded. (Guess that's one thing I have in common with my Deadbeat Dad, huh?)

Mr. Balloon handed me a couple of tickets and then he left. Actually, it was kind of like he disappeared. I turned around to give Matty the tickets and when I turned back, he was gone. Probably just ducked back into his booth—but it was still pretty creepy the way he was there one second and not there the next. ~~I didn't give it much thought at the time. But later, after It Happened, I couldn't stop thinking about~~

Anyway, Saint Matt was happy as a clam . . . and if he was happy, so was I. Shows you how dumb I was . . .

... doesn't it?

Took me ten minutes to get the dim bulb ticket taker to even understand what had happened.

He kept telling me that Matt was probably just playing a game, and I kept telling him that *my brother doesn't play games like that,* he—

Hey, look: what's the point of even going *over* this? I mean it was *five years ago.*

KATIE...?

KLIK

Might as well be a *lifetime.*

DON'T YOU KNOW I *HATE* IT WHEN YOU DO THIS?

DO *WHAT?* WHAT DO YOU *THINK?* HIDE IN THE *CLOSET.*

I *WASN'T* HIDING. I *LIKE* IT IN HERE.

IT'S THE ONLY PLACE IN THIS WHOLE STUPID APARTMENT WHERE I CAN GET SOME *PRIVACY.*

NOW HOW ABOUT SHUTTING THE *DOOR* AND LEAVING ME *ALONE?*

OUT.

YOU'RE A *TYRANT*.

I'M YOUR *MOTHER*. AND I'VE WORKED *HARD* ALL DAY AND I'M *TIRED* AND I'M IN *NO MOOD* FOR--

WHAT'S THAT?

A *DIARY?*

NOTHING.

YOU'RE KEEPING A *DIARY?*

OH, THAT'S *WONDERFUL*. I'M *SO* GLAD YOU TOOK DR. FRAYDA'S SUGGESTION TO HEART AND--

FIRST OF ALL, DR. FRAYDA IS AN *IDIOT*...AND IF YOU THINK I'M *EVER* GOING BACK TO SEE THAT STUPID SHRINK AGAIN *YOU'RE A BIGGER IDIOT*.

D RATHER MP OUT OF E *WINDOW* AN LET HER SS AROUND MY *HEAD* NY MORE.

SECOND OF ALL, THIS *ISN'T* A DIARY. THESE ARE MY *MEMOIRS*...AND WHEN *YOU'RE* OLD AND GRAY AND SENILE I'M GONNA HAVE THEM *PUBLISHED*--

--AND THEN THE *WHOLE WORLD* WILL KNOW *ALL* OUR DARK AND DIRTY SECRETS.

WHY DO YOU *SAY* THESE THINGS, KATIE? DO YOU ACTUALLY *ENJOY* HURTING ME?

HOW *LONG'S* IT GONNA TAKE YOU TO GET THAT I *DON'T* WANT YOU TO CALL ME *KATIE* ANY MORE. MY NAME IS *KATE*. K-A-T--

I KNOW HOW TO *SPELL* IT.

NOT *AGAIN*...

OT AGAIN WHAT?

YOU'RE STILL PUTTING THESE STUPID *POSTERS* UP?

HEY'RE OT--

Y'KNOW, SOMETIMES I FEEL LIKE I'M LIVING IN A *CRYPT*.

I MEAN, YOU HAVEN'T CHANGED *ANYTHING* IN HIS ROOM SINCE HE—

IT WAS *YOUR* ROOM, TOO.

A LONG *TIME* AGO.

IN CASE YOU HAVEN'T NOTICED, *I* SLEEP ON THE *COUCH*.

. . . and she's still at it. Never during the day or anything (she's actually managed to hold on to the same job for a couple of years. Some kind of dumb real estate thing), but she comes home after work and needs a drink to relax before dinner. A drink to unwind after dinner. A glass of wine before bed. When she can't sleep.

I still can't figure out what good it does her. It's not like she's any less wretched when she's drinking. It's not like she forgets the past five miserable years of her life. (Come to think of it, the years before that weren't exactly great either, were they?) No, she drags herself to bed every night and wakes up in the morning looking more depressed than the day before. And looking at me like it's my fault or something. I liked it a lot better when she was crying on the toilet.

Hey, I'm not stupid. I know why she does it: it's all because of my brother (and, okay, I'm not the easiest person in the world to live with)—but I meant what I said to Frances: Matt was gone. Gone forever.

And it was time to get over it.

May 19th. I've been thinking about something that I have to get straight. What I said to my mother was true: I'm not writing in this diary because of anything Dr. Frayda said (okay, so I admit it, they're not memoirs. But don't tell Frances. And, hey, you never know, maybe one day I really WILL publish them, and wouldn't that be cool?). I'm writing this because I want to. Because somebody's gotta tell the truth around here. And I guess it's got to be me.

(By the way, if you've never been to a shrink, consider yourself lucky. All they do is sit there and smile a Super-Fake Smile . . . except for when they're pretending to be Serious and Caring . . . and ask you idiotic questions. I've only been to Dr. Faker four or five times—and usually I'd just stare at her like SHE was the nutcase. Once in a while I'll make up answers to her dumb questions, like the time she asked me if I had any close friends and I told her I was pen pals with a convict who was sent to jail for murdering his therapist.)

Frances is the real wacko around here, but she's never gone to a shrink. Figures, right? But of course she's the one who's always telling me to "get in touch with my feelings" . . . which is a joke because she's so NOT in touch. If she was, she wouldn't spend so much time falling asleep in front of the TV. Or going out with losers who still wear ponytails and reek of cologne that smells like incense.

The joke is, most of the losers don't ever come back for a second date. How sad is that? I mean, Herbert the Great is out there somewhere having the time of his life . . . and Frantic Frances can't even get a twit with a ponytail to stick around?

Another reason why I'm writing this—and this is just between us—is because I don't exactly have any friends (no, not even in jail).

Oh, I hang around with some kids at school sometimes and maybe we'll go to a movie on the weekend. Or once in a while . . . but not very often, I'll tell you that . . . somebody'll invite me to sleep over at their house. But most of them are pretty much two-faced jerks. The minute you leave the room, you just know they're talking about you. And there's this one girl, Fiona, who's always asking me questions about my family—like it's so fascinating to her that my mother's psychotic, my father's a deadbeat, and my brother's face is on a milk carton. (Well, Fiona USED to ask me questions.

I finally told her to mind her own stinking business and never talk to me again and now when she sees me coming down the hall she just looks the other way. Which is just fine with me.)

Hey, look, it's not like I'm dying to go to stupid parties with a bunch of mental defectives who think that giggling is the height of conversation. But sometimes I wouldn't mind having just one person to talk to. ("Talk to Doctor Frayda," my mother always says. But, really, how pathetic is it when someone charges a hundred dollars an hour just to pretend to be your friend?)

So I guess that's why I write in this memoir, or diary, or whatever it is. I don't have to do it. I mean, when you think about it, it's really a major waste of time, right? I don't even know who I'm writing to. Myself, I guess. Which, when you think about it, is BEYOND pathetic.

May 22nd. So there's this old woman who's been living across the hall since dinosaurs ruled the Earth. I never see her much (once in a while I'll bump into her on the way to the incinerator or down at the mailboxes), but I can always hear her, whenever I go out or come in. Peering through the peephole, watching me.

Guess when people get that old (and Mrs. Vaughn is so ancient she looks like she's been dead for fifty years), their lives are so boring that the only thing they can do to stay interested is watch soap operas on TV and spy on their neighbors.

Anyway, the other day I'm coming home from school and just as I'm going in the house, I hear Mrs. Vaughn messing with the locks on her door. (Old people have a lot of locks. Guess they're afraid that someone's gonna break in and steal their false teeth or something.) Next thing I know she's poking her face out through the crack and hissing at me like some senile snake: "PSSSST! PSSSST!"

I thought about pretending I didn't hear her, but I didn't want to be rude (I figure when people get to that age, being weird's not their fault anymore). So, dumb me, I asked her what she wanted. She opened the door some more, said, "I want you, little lady!" and then—no kidding!—she grabbed me by the arm and dragged me into her apartment! I still don't know how she did it—I mean, my backpack alone weighs like five hundred pounds—but, before I knew what was happening, that old pterodactyl yanked me inside and locked the door behind us.

So now I'm seriously mad. "What's the big idea?" I said. And she flashed me this goofy smile (well, maybe it wasn't so goofy. Maybe it was kind of sweet. But in a really goofy way) and said, "Not so big. Just tea." I looked at her like she was totally crazy—which I was pretty sure she was—and then she said, "You drink tea, don't you? You eat cookies?" I said yeah, I guess so. And the next thing you know, she's got the teapot out and I'm sitting next to her on the couch. The cushions were so old I was sinking halfway to Middle-earth.

Why did I stay? I really don't know. Maybe I needed a couple of cookies to cheer me up. Y'see my grade adviser, Mrs. Stern (and, boy, was she ever), had called me down to her office that afternoon. I thought she was going to give me the old "You're a smart girl and I know you can try harder" speech— but it turned out to be the "How would you like to spend another year in the ninth grade?" routine instead. To tell you the truth, I didn't expect that.

Mrs. Vaughn's house had that old person smell. You know, like everything in it was preserved in plastic since 1950. My Gramma Esther's apartment smelled the same way.

(Gramma Esther died like a month after Herbert The Great ditched us. Did I mention that one? Great timing, huh?) It was actually kind of nice, that smell. In a disgusting, *Mummies from Beyond the Grave* sort of way.

I still miss my Gramma. So I guess I went brain-dead and started thinking that maybe Mrs. Vaughn got as lonely as Gramma used to.

Figured, hey—where's the harm in eating a couple of cookies (they were kind of stale, like old lady cookies always are, but they still tasted pretty good) and brightening her otherwise dark and dismal existence? So we were sitting there and nobody was saying anything and I was sinking deeper and deeper into the couch and thinking what a supremely dumb idea it was to get myself into this, when all of a sudden Mrs. Vaughn leaned in a little closer (I could smell her breath. It was kind of stinky, but kind of sweet at the same time. And that reminded me of my Gramma, too) and said how it had been a while since we'd had a chat. I told her I didn't think we'd ever had a chat. And she said, "Then we're long overdue."

And then she stared at me. For a reallyreallyREALLY long time. And I just sat there like a complete doofus smiling back at her (y'know, one of those frozen smiles like the Joker in the old Batman movie?) because, well, I didn't know what else to do. And then I saw the cabinet.

Mrs. Vaughn looked over at me and made this sound: "Ahhhh." But it was more than just "Ahhhh." It was like she'd been waiting her whole life to get that "Ahhhh" out. She sat there for a couple of seconds, then let it roll again: "Ahhhh . . ." And then, finally, she said: "I see you've noticed my mementos."

I was up off the couch in a shot. How could I not notice? I mean, there, in that banged-up old cabinet, was the most amazing collection of Abadazad stuff I'd ever seen.

It was like an Abadazad museum. There were copies of the first three books . . . *Little Martha in Abadazad*, *Queen Ija of Abadazad*, and *The Eight Oceans of Abadazad* . . . that looked as old as Mrs. Vaughn. A tiara that looked just like the one the Two-Fold Witch wore (I'm sure the rubies were fake, but they sure seemed real to me. Of course I've never seen a real ruby in my life). And, best of all, hand-painted figurines of Queen Ija, Professor Headstrong, Mary Annette, Mister Gloom, Master Wix, and a whole mess of other characters. And they weren't like the plastic junk you see in the toy stores. They weren't even like those ridiculously expensive "collectibles" they sell to super-nerd adults who never got a life. This stuff—I wish I could explain it—it was like they weren't based on the characters, they WERE the characters. Like each of those little figures had . . . I dunno . . . a soul or something.

And here's something I still don't understand: they didn't really look like the Abadazad characters, at least not the way Arthur N. Pierson drew them in the books. Some of them didn't resemble the Pierson versions at all. And yet they were just perfect the way they were. They—

Look, I told you before I'm not really into Abadazad anymore. It's kid stuff and I gave up kid stuff a long time ago. But looking at all that cool junk—I FELT like a little kid again. To tell you the truth, it's kind of embarrassing thinking about it now. But, embarrassing or not, that's how it was and if you don't like it you can stop reading right now, okay?

So, anyway, I'm standing there like a jerk with my mouth hanging open and Mrs. Vaughn said, "Really something, isn't it? You'll never find anything like it anywhere in the world."

"What is this," I asked her, "stuff you've been saving since you were a kid? I thought we had all the Abadazad garbage ever made. I've never seen anything like this."

Mrs. Vaughn flashed me that sweet/goofy smile again and said: "That's 'cause they're real."

"Excuse me?"

"They're real," she repeated. I could tell by her voice that she actually believed it. "Straight from Queen Ija's palace in the Floating City of Inconceivable."

That's when I knew I'd taken a left turn

into Loony Land. Right away I'm planning my escape. No way I was staying locked up in that apartment with some wrinkled head case. Meanwhile, the old wacko reaches into the cabinet and pulls out this blue ball. It was sitting on a pedestal that looked like it was made out of gold. (I'm sure it was as bogus as the rubies in the tiara.) The ball must've had some battery-powered light inside it because it was GLOWING . . . and when Mrs. Vaughn held it up, that light kind of danced across her face like Tinker Bell. I looked in her eyes and there were tears there. I don't know why—but, all of a sudden, I kind of felt like crying, too. (That scared me a little bit, because I don't cry. Ever. ~~Except once in a while when I'm watching sappy movies or thinking about~~ So it got me wondering if maybe her craziness was catching or something.)

"You know this," Mrs. Vaughn said, not taking her gaze off the ball, "the Blue Globe. Enchanted by the Two-Fold Witch herself. And if your heart is pure enough, true enough— and if you know the Magic Words—it will carry you, in less than a second, over the Eight Oceans . . . and into ABADAZAD."

I started backing toward the door. "Gee,"
I said, "it really is getting late. My mom . . .
she's like a mega-worrier and if I don't—"

She didn't miss a beat. Just put down
the globe, grabbed her ancient copy of
Little Martha in Abadazad, and said, "See
that?" She was pointing to the picture on
the cover. "That's me."

I couldn't help myself. I just had to ask:
"Who's you?"

"Her," she said.

"LITTLE MARTHA?"

"Martha Cooper. That was my name
before I married the late and much-lamented
Mr. Vaughn . . . but when I was a little girl,
everyone called me Little Martha."

I've gotta admit that, as tempted as I was
to dial 911 and have the Men in the White
Coats cart Mrs. Vaughn away, when I realized
that she really thought she was Little Martha
from the Abadazad books, well, I was totally
fascinated—in a morbid kinda way. (That's
Frances's favorite word for me: morbid. Once
she even introduced me as "My morbid
daughter." I really liked it.)

Know how, when you drive by some
horrible car accident or the kid who sits

next to you in class has just thrown up all over her desk, you really don't wanna look, but a part of you just HAS to? I guess it was like that. Which is why, like a dummy, I asked Mrs. Vaughn to tell me all about it.

She got this look like she was remembering something that made her incredibly happy and broke her heart, both at the same time. (I understand how someone could feel that way. When I think about Matty, it's the same thing.)

Look, I don't claim that every word I'm writing down is exactly the way it happened . . . it's not like I've got some kind of photographic memory . . . but this part of the conversation totally stuck in my head. Not because I believed her—I'm not a COMPLETE moron, thank you—but when someone, even someone as loony as Mrs. Vaughn, is talking about something that they believe with all their heart . . . well, you can't help but get caught up in it, y'know? Maybe it isn't true, but it sure is a great story. (And sometimes I think a great story can be more real than the truth.)

"It was a long time ago," Mrs. Vaughn said, "and a very different world. When I had my adventures in Abadazad . . . well, let's just say people weren't ready for books about a little Negro girl. That's what they called us back then, you know . . . Negroes. Guess it was better than some of the OTHER names they used." She shook her head and, for a couple of seconds, her eyes got a little . . . harder, I guess. Then she just sighed and swept her hand in front of her face, like she was shooing away a fly. "So," Mrs. V. went on, "when I met dear sweet Mr. Davies and told him my tale— well, things being what they were, he changed me . . . well, the character that he based on me . . . into a little white girl."

"Mrs. Vaughn," I piped up (couldn't keep my big mouth shut), "the first Abadazad books came out over a hundred years ago."

"Certainly did."

"But that would make you—"

"I'll be one hundred and fifteen years old this coming September."

"EXCUSE me?—"

"You see, time, as we know it, doesn't exist in Abadazad. You don't age while you're there. Not a day. Not an instant! And I was there, Katie—"

"Kate," I interrupted (yeah, yeah, I should've just shut up and let her talk, but, in case you haven't noticed, it drives me up the wall when people call me that. Not that it mattered, she wasn't even listening to me.)

"—for years and years. But adulthood tugs on a person. We're all so desperate to grow up—heaven only knows why. I finally left Abadazad. Didn't really regret it. Much. After all, I had fifty-three wonderful years with Mr. Vaughn." She stopped for a second . . . then did that shooing thing again with her hand. "But he's gone now . . . and I'll be gone soon, too. I can feel it in what's left of my bones."

When she said that, about her being gone, I felt a little sad. Maybe I was thinking about Gramma Ethel. What it was like at the end when she was so sick she could hardly move or talk or anything. I wanted to say something to make Mrs. Vaughn feel better, but all I could come up with was, "Yeah, well . . ."

That was brilliant, right? "I'm sorry if—"

She didn't even let me finish: "Nothing to be sorry about," she said, "'cause Queen Ija and the Two-Fold Witch told me that when my time came I'd be with them— reborn as a young girl again!—in Abadazad. And, oh—how my heart ACHES for that day."

She closed her eyes then. Kinda drifted off into her own head. I thought about saying something to her—but, really, what do you say to someone like that? Imagine if you met some loopy old geezer who swore he was the real Pinocchio . . . what're you gonna tell him? Good luck with the nose job and give my best to Jiminy Cricket?

So I just tiptoed toward the door. I managed to get it open and I was almost out in the hall when, all of a sudden, Mrs. Vaughn came up behind me, pushed the door closed, and whispered, "Your brother is alive."

I felt like somebody punched me in the chest. There was no way she could've said what I thought she'd said, right? I managed to grunt a "What?" and she shoved her face so close to mine that I could see all the little hairs on her chin.

"Matt's alive," she said, louder this time. "He's been kidnapped by the Lanky Man. Old Lanks found a way to cross over into our world. He's been stealing children— pure-hearted children like your brother—and heaven only knows what he intends to do with them."

I don't know exactly what happened to me then. I started shaking all over. My face got all hot. And I had this feeling, in the pit of my stomach, like I wanted to puke or scream or punch something. But I couldn't do anything. I could hardly talk. All I could croak out was, "That's not funny."

"No," Mrs. Vaughn said. "No, it's not. Not funny at all."

She put her hand on my arm. Her fingers were all twisted and bony, but there was something so gentle about the way she touched me. Like she knew she'd upset me and wanted to calm me down . . . but that only made me madder. I tried to pull away— but my heart was pounding and my body just wouldn't move. All I could do was listen.

"If I was younger," she said, "I would've sniffed the old devil out sooner . . . but I'm not good for much these days. Oh, but you . . . I'll help you get to Abadazad. You'll tell Queen Ija and she'll find your brother . . . she'll FIND him, Katie . . . and she'll stop Lanky from—"

When she called me Katie again . . . that stupid little girl name . . . I got so mad all the feeling in my body came back. I yanked my arm away. Mrs. Vaughn kind of stumbled back (for a second I thought she was gonna fall) and—I just couldn't help it—started yelling at her.

"Listen, lady," I screamed, "you wanna live in some warped little fantasy world—imagine you're somebody you're not—fine—go ahead. But leave me out of it!" I don't know what kind of reaction I expected. Guess I thought she'd start yelling back at me. Or kick me out of her house. Or maybe start howling like a werewolf. But she didn't do any of that. She just kind of sank into herself . . . the same way I sank into her couch. And she didn't say a word. Just stared at me like what I said had hurt her. Hurt her worse than anybody'd ever hurt her before.

I slammed the door and left.

I feel bad about it now . . . but only a little. She deserved it. She really did. I mean who does she think she is telling me Matt's alive, and in ABADAZAD, for crying out loud? What kind of twisted sicko says something like that, huh? I don't care how old you are or how lonely or crazy, NOBODY'S got the right to say that kind of stuff.

Tonight, when I was sitting at the dinner table sulking, Frances asked me what was wrong. I almost told her, too. I think maybe I wanted to. But somehow the words "Why don't you just mind your own business and leave me alone?" came out instead.

Frances got up, tossed her plate in the sink, and left the room. Some mother I've got, huh? Some life.

should never underestimate the power of an outraged little girl.) Utilizing the key she wore always 'round her neck, Martha undid the lock and rummaged beneath the neatly folded clothes until she found a secret compartment, within which was hidden a most extraordinary Globe. Molded of a glasslike substance bluer than the bluest sea, it rested atop a golden base upon which were scratched strange and beautiful symbols, like secret messages from the angels.

Both hands placed firmly upon the Blue Globe (which seemed to gently vibrate and hum, as if warmly greeting an old friend), Little Martha closed her eyes tight and, speaking not so much with her tongue as with her heart, intoned the following:

"I summon Queen Ija and the Two-Fold Witch to carry me to that Place where sorrow has no home, where time has no meaning, where joy lives forever!" And then seven times she proclaimed a word that was far more than a word, a name that was beyond all names: "Abadazad! Abadazad! Abadazad! Abadazad! Abadazad! Abadazad!

May 30th. I think. But I'm not really sure. If I told you WHY I'm not sure and where I AM right now you'd understand—but your brains might explode right out your ears. So I think maybe it'd be better if I just told you a little bit at a time, okay? Kind of ease you into it. (See? I'm pretty considerate when I wanna be.)

So where was I? Oh, yeah—Mrs. Vaughn. It was maybe a week after we had our little run-in. I'd just finished dinner (two bowls of cereal and five chocolate chip cookies: when Frances works late it's not exactly gourmet dining at our house). I could hear people running and shouting and doors opening and closing . . . so I went over to the peephole and looked out.

There were a bunch of nervous-looking EMT guys and they were wheeling a stretcher out of the old lady's apartment. It was like in the movies, y'know—when they've got the sheet pulled over the dead body? Only this time the dead body was real—and not some actor pretending to be dead.

My first thought was maybe somebody who'd been visiting Mrs. V. had croaked . . . but I knew that no one ever visited her, and besides I could hear Fat Mr. Potenza, the super, talking to Miss Epstein, the skinny dancer who lives in 308, telling her that Mrs. Vaughn had had a heart attack or a stroke or something.

"Poor old thing," Mr. Potenza said. And the way he said it made me want to go out in the hall and poke him in his blubbery belly and tell him that Mrs. Vaughn wasn't a thing, she was a PERSON. But I didn't.

I wasn't at the hospital when Gramma Esther died (Frances made me go to school that day and I'll never forgive her for that). At the funeral they had the casket closed up (part of me was upset about that, but part of me was relieved, too), so I'd never actually seen a dead person before.

I guess with Mrs. Vaughn all covered up like that I still haven't seen one . . . but when they wheeled her away I got a quick glimpse of her feet sticking out from the bottom of the sheet. She was wearing these faded old polka-dot socks. One of them had a hole in it . . . and her big toe was poking through.

I don't know what it was about that toe but the second I saw it my stomach turned inside out and the next thing I knew I was in the bathroom upchucking Rice Krispies and Famous Amos. (And if you think that's disgusting to read about, believe me, it was more disgusting to do.)

By the time that was over there was nobody out in the hallway anymore, so I ran over to the window and saw the ambulance pulling out. It was raining pretty hard but a bunch of people were standing around in front of the building and I thought maybe I should too—only I couldn't really figure out WHY I should. I mean, what good would it do? And anyway, even if she wasn't a hundred and fifteen years old like she claimed, Mrs. Vaughn was pretty ancient and old people die—just ask my Gramma—so, really, what was the big deal? Who was gonna care that there was one less crazy old lady in the world? Not me.

I had homework, but I decided to skip it. (Believe it or not, I actually do my homework. Once in a while. When I can't come up with a good excuse. But I figured having your neighbor drop dead was a fantastic excuse . . . and, besides, I still felt pretty limp from throwing up.) So I plopped down on my bed (if you can call a broken-down foldout couch a bed) and figured I'd just channel surf for a while.

I'd been watching TV for about fifteen minutes when I heard a knock at the door. Figured it was Frantic Frances forgetting her keys again, but when I opened the door there was nobody there. I was just about to go back in when I noticed a box on the floor, wrapped up in brown paper.

Usually when the mail lady or the UPS guy drop off packages they leave them with Fat Mr. Potenza. And then Fat Mr. Potenza—who also happens to be Extremely Lazy Mr. Potenza—calls us on the phone and tells us to come down to his apartment (which reeks of cigar smoke and BO, and if you've ever seen his kitchen you'd know the guy hasn't washed a dish since Bill Clinton was president) and get it. He'd never put down his remote control and bring it upstairs and, if he did, believe me, he'd be standing at the door with his hand out, waiting for a tip. He wouldn't just leave it there and go.

But, hey, they say miracles happen some-times . . . and I figured maybe the guy had the package with him when he came up to see about Mrs. Vaughn and left it outside the door then. Thing is, Fat Mr. Potenza was standing out in front of the building when I'd looked out the window earlier . . . I took another look and he was still there . . . and somebody'd just knocked on my door.

Look, I'm not Nancy Drew and I don't watch *Unsolved Mysteries* and it's not like the box was for me anyway so I really didn't care. The only packages we ever get are filled with junk my mother buys from catalogues and then returns when she realizes we can't afford it.

So I took the thing inside and that's when I noticed that it wasn't from J. Jill, or The Sharper Image, or Nordstrom, or anybody. There were no addresses at all . . . just a note taped to the side with the words FOR KATE written out in handwriting a heckuva lot neater than mine.

FOR KATE? Who'd leave a package for me? It sure wasn't Frances's handwriting and, really, there weren't very many people on the planet who liked me enough to say hello let alone leave a Mystery Box outside my door.

But, y'know, when I tore that note off and really looked at it, I had the strangest feeling. I knew that the box was from Mrs. Vaughn, I just knew it (don't ask me how). But if it was—who put it there? Who knocked on the door?

All of a sudden, I was getting the Major Creeps. In fact I almost went out in the hall and stuffed the box in the incinerator . . . and I would have, too—except that I knew, I just knew (don't ask me HOW!), what was inside. And I was right. It was the globe Mrs. Vaughn showed me in her apartment. THE BLUE GLOBE.

I picked it up and turned it over and over in my hands. The light was so bright, so beautiful—and yet I couldn't find a battery compartment or an on/off switch. I checked out the gold pedestal and, when I looked close, I could see writing all around the base. But the letters didn't look like anything I'd ever seen before. More like the ancient ~~hirogliffs hairogliphs~~ hieroglyphs (okay, so I looked it up) we read about in social studies.

I don't know how long I sat there on the floor staring at the thing. It kind of felt like I was in a trance or dreaming or something— 'cause I could swear the Globe was, well, talking to me. Only it wasn't talking to ME me, it was talking to some part of me I never even knew was there. Tugging at my mind . . . trying to make me remember. No, that's not right. It didn't want me to remember. It wanted me to know that there was something Really Important I'd NEVER FORGOTTEN.

I could kinda feel it, too—swimming up from the bottom of my thoughts. Something huge and bright and warm and—

Then I heard somebody laugh. At least I thought I did—but when I looked around, there was nobody there. I mean, who could be? Frances was still at work, and even if she was home she wouldn't be laughing at me, would she? Not unless she saw me sitting on the floor like a drooling idiot, playing with that toy globe.

And suddenly that's exactly what it seemed like—a silly toy. I flashed on being five or six when Herbert the Great got me a "Queen Ija Blue Globe" at Toys "R" Us. He was trying to buy my affection, I guess. I used to stare at that thing for hours, chanting magic words, hoping that I'd be whisked away to Abadazad. (Which, for the record, I never was.) And here I was, fourteen years old, doing the same stupid thing.

I figured upchucking my dinner must have rattled my brains around big-time . . . so after I was done calling myself every synonym for imbecile I could think of, I stuffed the globe back in its box and shoved it on the top shelf of the hall closet. Figured maybe I could take it down to Phil's Fantasy Universe (that's a store a few blocks up Seventh that—aside from smelling worse than Fat Mr. Potenza's apartment—sells manga and science fiction books and every toy or game the Hobbitt-heads, Star Warts, and Abadanerds could ever want). Maybe I'd get a few bucks for it.

So while I'm up on top of a stool with my lungs full of mothballs, I hear Frances's key in the door. She comes marching in, throws her bag down on a chair, and doesn't even say hello or anything. Just gives me one of THOSE LOOKS (y'know, the kind the executioner gives you before he lops off your head) and says, "You wanna explain this?"

I could see right away what she was holding—a letter from my guidance counselor, the stern Mrs. Stern, that I swiped out of the mailbox the day before and stuffed in the kitchen trash can. (Guess I didn't stuff it far enough.) I bet she'd been waiting all day for the chance to wave it in my face.

I knew I was sunk but I had to say something, so I tried "Hey, that's mine!" (I knew it was lame the minute it came out of my mouth, but, under the circumstances, it was the best I could do.)

"Funny," Frances said, "it's addressed to me."

"I threw that away," I yelled (sometimes if I yell loud enough Frances will get exasperated and leave the room, which buys me time to come up with some better excuses), "and you had no right to—"

"Fish my own letter out of the trash?" Frances said. She didn't look like she was going anywhere.

"Look," I said, figuring I'd better try another strategy, "Mrs. Stern hates me. Anything she says in there is a total lie."

"So," Frances said in that smug voice she uses when she knows she's got me cornered, "you haven't been cutting classes? You're not failing math and science and social studies?"

Arguing clearly wasn't going to work . . . so I thought I'd try the Patented Kate Jameson Glare. That's when I fold my arms over my chest and give my opponent the Evil Eye.

Let her know that I'm not to be messed with. One false move and I'll incinerate her with my steely gaze.

But the Glare was a dismal failure with Frances (mainly because I forgot she was the one who patented it in the first place). She just sat on my bed and said, "Katie—" She corrected herself before I could bite her head off. "Kate . . . look. We can't go on like this. I love you, sweetheart. I haven't been the perfect mother . . . let's face it, I haven't even come close . . . but God knows I've done my best."

I couldn't argue with that. I mean, her best may have stunk—but it didn't change the fact that she'd given it everything she had. I was maybe gonna tell her, too—but all I could say was, "Yeah, well . . ." I think she knew what I meant. At least I hope she did.

Frances sat down on my bed next to me. "Tell me what to do," she said—and she sounded beyond tired. Like having me for a daughter had pretty much drained every last drop of her blood. "Tell me how I can help you."

"I don't need any help from you." And I didn't need it. Although maybe, right then, I wanted it. I sort of slid my hand across the sheet, just to get a little closer in case she got the urge to, I dunno, hold it or something. And she did.

But then she opened up her big mouth and ruined everything: "Look, sweetie," she said, "I don't have to be Dr. Frayda to know how much guilt you're still carrying around over—"

What was she talking about? Guilt? Me? SHE was the one who wasn't around when Matt needed her! And I told her so, too: "I was ALWAYS there for him! ALWAYS!"

I got right in her face then. I'd been waiting five years to get this out and she was gonna hear every rotten word. "Maybe," I said, "if you weren't such a screwup, he'd still be here—you ever think of that?"

It was kind of spooky. She didn't get mad. She didn't try to defend herself. She just looked me right in the eyes and said, "All the time." Then she went in her bedroom and locked the door.

Did I feel bad for what I said? Sure. Contrary to popular belief I'm not TOTALLY made of stone. But it was true, wasn't it?

So there I was, eleven o'clock at night, sitting in a giant *soap bubble*... *floating* over Ocean Avenue. Which meant one of *two things:*

Either I was *sleeping*—and this was the *weirdest* dream I'd ever had...

...or I was *completely demented*.

I *pinched* myself a couple of times to see if I'd *wake up*. Nothing happened.

Then (just for a second) I actually thought of calling *Doctor Frayda*...

...y'know, just to see if she had any advice for a kid whose *mind* had just melted all over the living room *floor*.

But all of a sudden (don't ask me *how*)...

...I knew *exactly* what to do.

I SUMMON *QUEEN IJA* AND THE *TWO-FOLD WITCH* TO CARRY ME TO THAT PLACE WHERE SORROW HAS *NO HOME*--

--WHERE TIME HAS *NO MEANING*... WHERE *JOY* LIVES *FOREVER!*

ABADAZAD!
ABADAZAD!
ABADAZAD!
ABADAZAD!
ABADAZAD!
ABADAZAD!
ABADA--

right do you have to come falling out of the sky scaring people half to death?"

"I," slurred the head-thing in a thick, dull voice, "am a Rocket Head. And it's my job to come falling out of the sky scaring people to death."

"Your job?" Little Martha replied. "Are you saying that someone has actually hired you to do such a terrible thing?"

"Indeed," rejoined the Rocket Head.

"Who?" challenged Martha.

The Rocket Head grinned, a fairly hideous sight, and spoke three words: "The Lanky Man." Martha didn't know what those words meant, but they made her uneasy. "Farewell," added the Rocket Head, in his drawling, indolent fashion.

"Farewell?" she inquired, now as confused as she was uneasy.

"Farewell," repeated the Rocket Head, who proceeded to explode into precisely eight hundred and forty-six pieces. Little Martha felt herself lifted off her feet and flung high into the air, tumbling end over end above the forest. She could have panicked; but, like her father, the eminent Colonel Cooper, Little Martha was both absurdly brave and ferociously practical. So even as

"ABSURDLY BRAVE AND FEROCIOUSLY PRACTICAL."

QUEEN IJA OF ABADAZAD

SO IT WAS WITH ONE GIRL.

Queen Ija OF ABADAZAD
BY FRANKLIN O. DAVIES

BUT HOW, I WONDER, WILL IT BE WITH THE OTHER?

SURELY, MY QUEEN, YOU ALREADY KNOW! YOU HAVE ONLY TO LOOK WITHIN TO SEE THE ANSWER!

NO ANSWER CAN BE MADE CLEAR—UNTIL THE PROPER QUESTION IS ASKED.

PROFOUND! INEFFABLE! EXTRAORDINARY!

I MUST RETURN TO MY ROOMS IMMEDIATELY IN ORDER TO SUFFICIENTLY PONDER THIS PENETRATING INSIGHT!

PONDER LATER, MY FRIEND. FOR NOW—CALL THE OTHERS.

WE HAVE MUCH TO DO— MUCH TO PREPARE—

—BEFORE OUR GUEST ARRIVES!

So one minute I'm in our apartment and the next . . .

. . . well, I didn't know where I was. Okay, okay—I pretty much knew right away where I was. It's not like you run into ten-foot-tall talking flowers at the Brooklyn Botanic Garden or animals that are part rabbit and part turtle in the Prospect Park Zoo. Only place I'd ever seen those things—they're called Sour Flowers and Shelloppers, by the way—was in Franklin O. Davies's books.

Which meant that maybe the crazy old lady across the hall wasn't so crazy. That the Blue Globe she gave me was the Real Deal and it had magically carried me over the Eight Oceans . . . and into Abadazad.

On the other hand, I'd taken that header out the living room window a few minutes before—so there was every chance I'd cracked my skull in half and I was really in an ambulance somewhere, hallucinating. Or maybe I was even dead.

Although I've got a feeling that if you're dead you pretty much know it. Doesn't seem like you'd have to guess about something like that. Which means I MUST have been hallucinating, right? Drifting along in some dumb fantasy my mind tossed together out of Davies's stories.

But if that was the case, how come the Shelloppers had disgusting breath (I'm talking major gross-out) and the Sour Flowers gave off a smell like an overflowing toilet? They never mentioned that in *The Edges of Abadazad.*

Edges was the seventh Abadazad book—and the only one Davies ever used those stupid characters in. No surprise. I mean, the Shelloppers were nauseatingly cute . . . and they talked in this

annoying rhyme that used to drive me nuts. Stuff like "Can we help you, little friend, can we take your hand? We'll go dancing far and wide across this magic land." See what I mean? Even Saint Matt couldn't stand it.

And the Sour Flowers? Worse. All they did was mope around and pout and burst out crying for no particular reason.

So, anyway, the Shelloppers were breathing their sewer-breath right in my face sniffing at me . . . and all of a sudden I realized I was still in my nightgown. (It's not a NIGHTGOWN nightgown. It's a Thrashing Plague T-shirt that I use as a nightgown. Thrashing Plague, by the way, is The Greatest Rock and Roll Band in The History Of The World, and if you've never heard of them, I seriously pity you.) And, stupid as it sounds, I started feeling kind of self-conscious and maybe a little embarrassed.

Then one of those stinks-worse-than-a-dead-cat Sour Flowers knocked the Shelloppers away . . . just swatted them with his arms or leaves or whatever they were . . . and started snarling at me. And all of a sudden I started thinking that the cute and boring versions from the books . . .

I'VE **GOT** TO BE DREAMING. THER THAT OR I'VE FINALLY ONE **TOTALLY** MENTAL.

DON'T YOU REMEMBER WHAT I **TOLD** YOU, DEAR? HOW **QUEEN IJA** AND THE **TWO-FOLD WITCH** WERE GONNA BRING ME BACK AFTER I DIED...MAKE ME A GIRL AGAIN--?

WELL, THEY WERE AS GOOD AS THEIR **WORD**!

AFTER YOU DIED. RIGHT. HOW COULD I FORGET?

I BET IF I **WAIT** A WHILE... I'LL WAKE UP. PROBABLY IN THE **HOSPITAL** WITH A BUNCH OF BROKEN BONES...BUT, HEY, **THAT'S** OKAY.

I CAN **DEAL** WITH THAT.

SWEETHEART, YOU'RE NOT **DREAMING.** YOU'RE NOT **CRAZY.** YOU'RE NOT IN ANY **HOSPITAL.**

YOU'RE JUST IN **ABADAZAD,** THAT'S ALL.

WELCOME **HOME.**

Then...I don't know **why**...but just for a second, I felt-- **happy,** I guess. At least I **think** it was happiness. Truth is, it'd been so long...

...I'd almost forgotten what it was like.

UH-OH.

EXCUSE ME FOR A MOMENT, DEAR.

TAKE YOUR **TIME.**

When I looked up in the sky, I saw something floating around up there, pretty far away. Just a shape, really . . . kinda vague . . . spinning through the clouds. At first I thought it was some kind of UFO—y'know, like the mother ship at the end of *Close Encounters*? But really it was more like a prism. The sun was reflecting through it and the colors (not the kind of colors we're used to. These were colors I'd never even imagined and, if I wrote a thousand pages, I could never describe) were so bright, so intense, that they made me dizzy and—

And then it was gone. Just sailed away across the sky. And it felt like a part of me kind of sailed away WITH it. I watched and watched till there wasn't even a hint of it left, then turned to Martha and asked, "Is that really . . . ?"

"Indeed it is," Martha said.

"And—Queen Ija's up there? Professor Headstrong? Mary Annette? Mr. Gloom?"

"ALL of them, Katie. And you can bet they'll help you find Matt . . . and free him from the Lanky Man."

She did it again, right? Called me Katie. And that's all it took.

Y'know when you're dreaming and all of a sudden you KNOW you're dreaming, even though you're still in it? Well, that's how I felt when I heard that stupid name again. Yeah, sure, I thought, I'm in Abadazad and we're gonna rescue my dead brother from some bad guy with pipe cleaner legs? Dream or not, it was all a bunch of garbage.

It had to be, right?

I turned to Little Miss Sunshine and said (well, shouted), "Hey, my name's not Katie, it's Kate—and my brother is dead! He died a long time ago!" The Shelloppers got scared then and ducked for cover. The Sour Flowers, on the other hand, leaned in closer like they were enjoying it. I didn't care. "Look," I said, "I don't know what's going on here . . . whether this is a nightmare . . . or some kind of pathetic, disgusting joke! But whatever it is—I DON'T WANT ANY PART OF IT!"

I just took off then—not that I had any clue where I was going—and Martha took off after me. "Kate," she called—at least she got it right that time—"please! A moment ago I saw your eyes . . . I saw your faith!

You believed! If there's even a chance that this is real, then you've got to come with me to Inconceivable!"

I was ready to shove her away and say something really nasty . . . I think you know by now that I'm pretty good at it when I wanna be . . . when she put her hand on my arm. And then—well, I'm getting chills just remembering it.

Martha touched me . . . and it didn't seem like some little girl. It seemed just like Mrs. Vaughn. I could almost feel those bony old fingers—and there was the same softness, the same, well, kindness that I'd felt back in her apartment. I swear, If I'd closed my eyes . . . I wouldn't have known the difference.

I stopped then . . . turned around and looked at Martha . . . really looked . . . and I had the same feeling about her eyes. Like they were MRS. VAUGHN'S EYES, stuck in a different face. And she was staring at me just the way Mrs. Vaughn did that afternoon she called me into her apartment. Like I'd hurt her in some way. Like she was depending on me—and I'd let her down.

I started feeling guilty then, although I can't say why . . . it's not like I'd done anything wrong (ever have that happen? You start feeling guilty about stuff, even when there's no reason? I hate that) and she was giving me That Look and I started thinking about what she said. Okay, so there was a pretty good chance that I was dreaming or dead or just plain nuts . . . but what if there was even the tiniest chance this was real? Didn't I owe it to Matty, to myself, to at least find out?

Well, anyway, what else was I gonna do? I was stuck there, I had to do SOMETHING.

"Yeah, okay," I finally agreed. "I'll go with you." Martha smiled . . . the same sweet/goofy smile Mrs. Vaughn had . . . and I almost smiled back. Then I thought better of it and sort of scowled instead (I'm not sure why. Guess so she knew I didn't actually trust her or anything). "But I don't have to like it."

So off we went, those dumb Shelloppers jumping up and down waving at us (at least they didn't start singing!), while the Sour Flowers stuck their tongues out and thumbed their noses (well, I guess they leafed their noses, since they didn't have thumbs).

I knew from the books that public transportation in Abadazad wasn't exactly like New York's. There were no buses or subways or yellow cabs. If we wanted to get up to the Capital City—we'd have to find a Living Staircase.

According to Martha (I couldn't bring myself to call her "Little" Martha. It's one thing to read a ridiculous name like that in book, but try actually SAYING it to someone), there was a Staircase Stop a couple of miles away . . . so off we trudged, across the fields and into the woods.

She kept chattering away—telling me how wonderful it was that I was there and how everyone at the Palace was expecting me and all kinds of other junk—and I kept telling her to be quiet, I didn't want to talk to any stupid hallucination.

"Even if I am a hallucination," Martha said, "is that any reason to be rude?" I told her it certainly was—but I didn't mean it. (I guess the real reason I didn't want to talk to her was because I kind of liked her . . . and how crazy was that? Liking someone who probably didn't even exist?)

The deeper in the woods we went, the

worse my mood got. Trees and dirt and bugs aren't exactly my favorite things. When I was in the Brownies (I was six or seven when I joined and I dropped out after three weeks) we went for a hike in Prospect Park, and every time a mosquito came near me I started screaming and flapping my arms like a total dope. And in Abadazad some of the bugs actually talk to you, which may be adorable in a cartoon but, believe me, the first time a worm tells you to "keep your chin up and have a SPLENDIFEROUS day" it's more like a horror movie.

On top of all that, I suddenly realized I was starving (warning: you do NOT want to be around me when my blood sugar gets low) and made sure Martha knew it. "Not to worry," she told me, "we'll be stopping for lunch any minute."

"Oh, really?" I snapped. "What're we gonna have . . . poisoned berries with a side order of dirt?"

"There are some trees up ahead that—"

"I don't eat things that grow on TREES," I barked, cutting her off. "I eat REAL food!"

Martha grinned like the Cheshire Cat. "You'll eat THIS," she said.

She was right. In a couple of minutes we found ourselves in this amazing grove of trees that were sprouting all kinds of food. I'm not talking about apples or oranges—these trees had pizza and hot dogs and hamburgers hanging from the branches. (Martha said they were Lunch Trees. "Don't you remember, Kate? From Book Five? *The Enchanted Gardens of Abadazad*?") Right across from the Lunchers were half a dozen Dessert Trees that were growing ice-cream cones and cookies and more cupcakes than I could count.

The thing I couldn't wrap my brain around was that the burgers and dogs tasted just like the ones at the Second Avenue Deli in Manhattan (every once in a while, just for a treat, Frances and I take the train in and have a pig-out lunch at the Deli, go to the movies, and then, for dinner, stuff ourselves with Indian food down on Sixth Street. Proof that my mother isn't ALWAYS a total drag) and the Dessert Trees had things like Twinkies—which were Matty's favorite—and those chocolate cupcakes with the white squiggle in the middle that I eat way too much of.

Martha explained that the way the trees worked was they sort of pick up on your thoughts, rooting around in your head to find out what foods you really love and, POOF!—there they are. So if I'd been, say, a vegetarian (which I definitely would be— except that I'm allergic to soy and I hate vegetables), I would have found tofu dogs and veggie burgers and those disgusting fruit-juice sweetened cookies Frances is always trying to force down my throat.

And, y'know, while I was stuffing my face (and stuffing my face and stuffing my face) I had to wonder: If none of this was real . . . how come I was so ravenous? And how come the food tasted so incredible?

It was a good thing I porked out because those "couple of miles" turned into like ten. And keep in mind I was barefoot and in my nightgown and I'm the kind of person who, if I've got to go more than a block, pleads and whines so my mother will drive me. (Okay, so we don't even have a car, but I figure if I beg her enough she might go out and buy one. Not that it's worked so far.) Anyway, it seemed like the more we walked, the darker and colder it got. My feet were blistering, my butt was freezing, my nose was running and I was not my Normal Happy Self. (No comments, please.)

Things got worse when we left the forest. Suddenly the ground was all dry and cracked and dusty. The trees (the few we saw) were gnarled and bare. And there were these rocks that . . . I know this is gonna sounds nuts (okay, after everything else I've told you, maybe not) . . . made me feel like they were watching me. When I finally got the courage to peek over at one of them . . . I saw eyes LOOKING BACK AT ME. Glaring. Kinda like the Patented Jameson Glare—only a lot worse. I jumped so high I think I broke some Olympic record. "Martha!" I said (okay, so I shrieked hysterically).

"What's wrong?" she asked.

"That rock! It just . . . LOOKED at me!"

"And . . . ?"

"Didn't you hear what I said? A ROCK was LOOKING at me!"

Martha sighed like one of my teachers when they think I should know the answer to a question and I haven't got the vaguest clue. "Kate, dear," she said, "the rocks DO that here."

"They do?"

"Of course they do. It is Abadazad, after all."

"Abadazad," I snorted, "right." Like that just explained everything. (Well, I guess it did.) "But, Martha . . . you should've seen the way it looked at me! It—"

Martha swept her hand in front of her face, like she was shooing away a fly (and it was a little spooky because I remembered Mrs. Vaughn doing the exact same thing). "Oh," she said, "don't pay any attention to that. They're just grouches." She shook her head and started walking again. "They don't like anybody."

Then one of them did it again—gave me the Evil Eye—and I ran, faster than I knew I could, to catch up with Martha. "They don't?" I asked.

"Why," Martha said, "the queen herself once came through on a Royal Expedition—and they even gave HER dirty looks!"

"Wow. She must've been mad, huh?"

"Oh, nobody can make Queen Ija angry. She sees the good in everyone."

"Yeah? Well, a couple of days in Brooklyn

would change that attitude pretty fast."

Martha just laughed then, slipped her arm through mine (I almost pulled away from her—then I realized I kind of liked it), and called me a "silly girl." I've been called all kinds of things—some of them I wouldn't even write down in this book—but never a "silly girl." I kind of liked THAT, too.

So we walked along, not really saying much, and it would have been pretty wonderful—it WAS pretty wonderful, for a little while. Thing is, I was totally exhausted, totally freezing, my feet hurt, and I reallyreallyREALLY had to go to the bathroom . . .

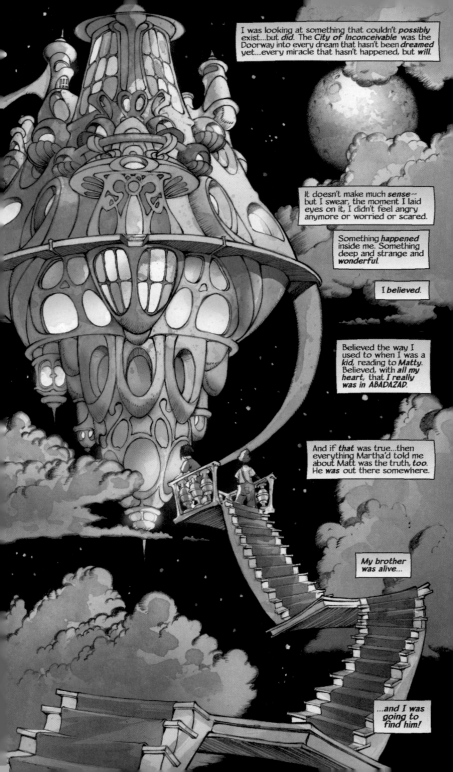

but his daughter was possessed of a questing mind and a daring heart, and she could occasionally—well, perhaps more than occasionally—be the cause of no small trouble at 362 Travers Place. The Colonel, having fought in many a distinguished battle in the Civil War, knew how to discipline Little Martha and yet, to his credit, did it without ever lifting a hand.

But these Lanky Boys, as their master called them, were wild, undisciplined and, worst of all, unloved. Most had been stolen from their families as infants, raised in the shadowy bowels of Old Lanks' hidden city, and put to work in his factories as soon as they could walk. How to explain, then, the devotion they showed their soulless "father"? How to explain the way they crowded about him, like hungry ants around a crumb of bread? Some things, dear reader, defy explanation; but if the author were to venture a guess, he would say that, to a child desperate for adult guidance, any attention is better than no attention at all. Even the attention of one so repugnant and cruel as the Lanky Man.

"Do you see," Old Lanks hissed to Little Martha, lining his boys up and displaying them for her as if they were toys on a shelf,

The Wretchedly Awful City of **ABADAZAD**
BY FRANCIS O. DAVIES

"REPUGNANT"? "CRUEL"?

NO MATTER *HOW* MANY TIMES I PERUSE THIS RUBBISH--I NEVER FAIL TO BE *PROFOUNDLY* INSULTED!

THEN...UH... HOW COME Y'KEEP *READIN'* IT...?

THERE ARE *TWO* REASONS--NOT THAT A FEEBLEMINDED, HALF-WITTED *DUNCE* LIKE YOURSELF COULD EVER UNDERSTAND THEM.

REASON NUMBER *ONE:* IT'S ABOUT *ME.*

REASON NUMBER *TWO:* STUDYING THESE ACCOUNTS-- HOWEVER *JAUNDICED--* OF MY ENCOUNTERS WITH THAT *INSUFFERABLE* LITTLE MARTHA--

--WILL HELP ME IN MY EFFORTS TO EVALUATE THE THREAT THIS *NEW* ARRIVAL POSES TO MY PLANS.

YOU SAYIN' YOU'RE...AFRAID OF SOME *LITTLE GIRL?*

STOP ASKING QUESTIONS, DODO! WE HAVE MUCH TO *DO*--MUCH TO *PREPARE*--

--IF WE'RE TO GIVE THE YOUNG LADY A...*PROPER* GREETING.

The Staircase dropped us off (*gently,* I'm happy to report) at the gates of the Royal Palace.

I guess a part of me was expecting crowds of people, bands playing, Mary Annette singing one of her crazy-brilliant songs (sort of like that scene at the end of the second Abadazad movie, after Princess Aji's been defeated and Queen Ija declares a Royal Holiday). But there wasn't a soul around. Nobody. Not even a talking bug.

Everything was really quiet. No, it was way more than just quiet. It was the deepest, the truest (that's the only way I can explain it: IT WAS TRUE) silence that ever existed.

And there were the gates towering above us—it seemed like they rose up for a mile!—studded with thousands of jewels that glittered in the moonlight. I heard some guy on TV once talking about the Promised Land. Well, I don't know what he meant, but it sure felt like that's where I was . . . because every one of those jewels was shining with a promise. A promise that nothing has to be the way we think it is. That everything can always be better. That everything WILL be better.

I looked over at Little Martha (all right—so maybe the name was growing on me) and, for the first time, she seemed . . . I don't know . . .

not scared, but—What's the word I'm looking for? Awed, I guess. Like, even after all those years, after all her incredible adventures—each time she came here was like the first. The magic of it . . . and the mystery . . . was always new.

And then the gates swung open.

"Who did that?" I whispered.

"They open themselves, dear," Martha whispered back. She grinned, held out her hand to me . . . I took it . . . and we walked in.

The hallway seemed to go on and on forever . . . and there still wasn't a soul in sight. The only light came from these . . . well, I'm not sure if they were some kind of crystals—or if they were alive. They made these musical sounds (imagine the most beautiful wind chimes you've ever heard and then multiply that beauty by ten) and they fluttered way up over our heads like butterflies. The Crystal-Chimers (Davies never wrote about them in the books—but that's what Martha called them) weren't much brighter than candles, but the light they gave off was warm, like the sun. Only this light didn't just warm your body—it warmed your heart.

I let go of Martha's hand . . . rushed up ahead . . . and smacked right into this humongoid statue. I swear it must have been twenty or thirty feet tall—but it was hard to tell exactly because the statue was floating in midair. Which made a lot of sense considering who it was a statue OF.

"That," I said, finding it hard to get the words out, "that's the Floating Warlock, right? Queen Ija's father." Martha nodded her head and said, "Not the same as he looked in Mr. Pierson's drawings, is he?"

"No," I agreed, "but you can tell it's him. You can feel it."

And I really could. It was as if it actually was the Floating Warlock himself—the Sorcerer-King who'd dreamed Abadazad into existence—magically appearing out the shadows just to welcome us.

And then I felt this incredible excitement . . . like the feeling you get on Christmas Eve, when you're imagining all the presents that'll be waiting for you in the morning. (The dreaming's always better than the presents. At least it works that way in MY house.) "Will I get to meet him?"

Martha got this ultraserious look on her face and said, "He's not here, Kate."

"Not here? Whaddayou mean?"

"A hundred years ago, as best we can measure time in a land where there IS no time, he went off on one of his quests. AND NEVER RETURNED."

"But he came back," I said. "In the last book of the series, he—"

Little Martha sighed. It wasn't an impatient kind of sigh, more of a disappointed one. "Wishful thinking on Mr. Davies's part, I'm afraid. But we never give up hoping." She did that flyshooing thing with her hand again then pointed up at the Crystal Chimers. "Come on, they want us to follow them."

So we walked for a couple more minutes—or maybe a couple more hours—and we eventually came to these drop-dead gorgeous double doors . . . pearl-white . . . in the shape of fairy wings.

Martha didn't have to tell me. I'd seen them in the books a gajillion times: these were the doors to Queen Ija's throne room.

"Well," Martha asked, "are you ready to go in?"

All of a sudden I didn't think it was such a good idea. "Go in?" I said. "Nuh-uh. I mean, what does a queen want to meet a loser like ME for?"

That's when I heard THE VOICE. Remember what I said before about it feeling like Christmas Eve? Well, this voice was Christmas Eve, Christmas morning, Easter, Halloween, the Fourth of July and your very best birthday— all rolled into one.

"You summoned me, Kate," the Voice said, "when you cradled the Blue Globe in your arms and spoke the invocation. You asked me to bring you here. It's too late to turn back now."

The wings started moving . . . the doors opened up . . . and suddenly there was all this LIGHT pouring out—like a thousand sunrises and a thousand sunsets blended together. Part of me was scared, I admit it. I wanted to run away. But the Voice was right: it WAS too late to turn back now.

So I took a deep breath, grabbed Martha's hand again (a little too tight, I think), stepped into the Throne Room . . . and there she was, hovering in her winged throne.

The Fairy Queen herself, Ija the First—ruler of all Abadazad.

Thing is, she WAS Ija—and she WASN'T. The queen I'd always read about was blond-haired and blue-eyed . . . not much older than me. But this Ija—well, at first I didn't even think she was human. It wasn't just the three eyes and the blue skin (which, let's face it, was weird enough), it was that she seemed . . . I dunno . . . ancient. Not in the way she looked—but in the way she felt. Like she was older than time. Older than everything.

"Come forward," Queen Ija said, but my legs just wouldn't move. Martha gave me a poke in the ribs with her elbow and I stumbled toward the throne, nearly falling in the queen's lap.

"Is something wrong, child?" she asked.

"Wrong?" I wanted to say. "Nope. What could be wrong? I'm walking around INSIDE A BOOK . . . only nobody actually looks like they did in the book . . . and the dead old lady in the little girl's body tells me you're gonna help me find my brother, who's been missing for five years. What could be wrong?"

That's what I wanted to say—but my lips
were suddenly as frozen as my legs had been.
All that came out of my normally humongous
mouth was this pathetic little squeak. Queen
Ija laughed (I think it was the nicest laugh I'd
ever heard. It sort of splashed all over me
like warm water) and then she said, "You've
had a long, confusing journey, Kate." (She didn't
call me Katie—not once—which made me like
her more than I already did. Which was a lot.)
"I want you to rest. We'll talk in the morning—
and all your questions will be answered."

"Rest sounds like a terrific idea, Your
Majesty." I'd never called anyone that before.
Hey, I'm an American. We don't have queens
and kings, and we sure don't like calling people
by fancy titles like Lord Pompous and Lady
Fullofherself. But for Ija it just seemed
perfect. I mean that's what she was: Her Majesty.
She couldn't have possibly been anything else.

So then Stupid Me gets carried away and
tries to curtsy because, y'know, that's what
you're supposed to do when you're with a
queen, right? Only thing is I'd never curtsied
before in my life . . . and I ended up falling on
my butt. Well, I WOULD'VE fallen on my butt if

Martha hadn't come up behind me and caught me. "Don't you dare laugh," I whispered.

"Wouldn't dream of it," Martha said . . . and then, of course, she did. Laugh I mean. And the truth is, it was sort of funny. In a painfully humiliating kind of way.

Then Ija gestured to Little Martha. "Come here, my dear old friend," she said. Martha didn't waste a second. She sprinted across that Throne Room like she was on the track team or something and jumped into the queen's lap. (Okay, I admit it: I was a little jealous. And you would be, too—so don't act so superior.)

The two of them just sat there for the longest time holding each other. Martha's face was buried in Her Majesty's shoulder. She was sobbing and sobbing and sobbing (or maybe laughing and laughing and laughing—sometimes it's hard to tell the difference) and Ija kept patting her head . . . stroking her hair. Then I noticed tears (they looked like liquid diamonds) trickling, shimmering, down the queen's cheeks and I realized (I mean, suddenly it was so incredibly obvious) that this was the first time the two of them had seen each

other since Martha . . . well, since she'd died
and been reborn here.

And there was so much love between
them, so much happiness, that I wasn't the
least bit jealous anymore. In fact seeing them
together like that started me thinking about
what it would be like seeing Matty again.

That should have made me happy, right? I
mean, there I was in Abadazad and, if what
Martha said was true (and why wouldn't it be?),
my brother was alive and, with the queen's help,
I was gonna find him and save him and—

"There's no such thing as happily ever after.
Haven't you figured that out by now?" I whipped
around to see who was talking—but there was
no one there except Ija and Martha. They were
still cooing and clucking over each other . . . and
all of a sudden it didn't seem so sweet and
wonderful anymore. In fact the two of them
were starting to get on my nerves.

"It's been five years," Whoever It Was
piped up again. "He's dead." I recognized that
voice. It was MY voice. Those were MY words.
"Get over it." My head started pounding the
way it does sometimes before a big test . . .
and my stomach was flopping around like a

fish. "He's dead," the voice . . . my voice . . . said again. (But if it was my voice, how come it wasn't coming from inside me? How come it sounded like it was coming from somewhere else in the room?)

Then I heard someone laughing (a really mean laugh that sounded familiar—but I couldn't remember from where), and I felt like—bear with me on this—like my mind was this gigantic stew pot and someone stuck a spoon in, stirring up all my doubts. I started thinking that this couldn't be real, that I couldn't possibly be standing in Queen Ija's Throne Room. "Matt's dead." Old ladies don't die and get reborn as little girls, and brothers don't get kidnapped by characters from hundred-year-old kids' books. "Get over it." The voice (my voice!) was banging at me like a drum: "Matt's dead, get over it, Matt's dead, get over it, Matt's—"

Queen Ija jerked her head up then, almost like she'd heard the voice, too. Before I knew what was happening, she'd put Martha back down and sailed her throne across the room straight at me—so fast I thought she was gonna knock me over. And the whole time Ija's staring at me. No, not at me . . . INSIDE me. Deeper

than I'd ever looked inside myself. All three of those eyes pushing through every thought and feeling . . . every memory and dream . . . I'd ever had. And ever WILL have.

It was like she was seeing the Real Me. Not the me I show to Frances or the creeps at school. Not even the me I show myself. THIS WAS THE ME THAT MATTY KNEW.

And that's what it felt like, y'know? It wasn't Queen Ija looking at me, it was my brother—looking through her eyes. Like wherever Matt was . . . she'd reached out to him somehow, pulled him close, let me see him there inside her . . . just for a moment. And then the moment was over. Matt was gone. But I knew he was alive. I knew there was hope.

I looked up at the queen. "Thank you," I started to say, "for showing—"

She didn't let me finish. "Doubt," Her Majesty said—and her voice was different somehow. Kind of like a thundercloud . . . huge and dark and maybe even a little dangerous. "Doubt," she repeated, "when used wisely can be a very useful tool. But left unchecked—" She raised her eyebrows, all three of them. "—it can undo the highest magic and transform even

the greatest kingdom—into an utter wasteland."
Then the thundercloud passed and Ija smiled—like
the sun coming out again after a big storm.
Martha walked over to me, grabbed hold of
my hand. Squeezed it.

"Good night, my darling girls," Queen Ija
said, blowing us each a kiss. "Sleep safely.
Sleep well."

The Throne Room's doors started to
open and we were almost out in the hall when
the queen called after me: "Kate."

I looked back. "Yes, Your Majesty?"

"You're forgetting something," she said.
Oh, great, I thought. What did I screw up now?

Ija smiled then (one of those *Mona Lisa* kind
of things . . . y'know, like she's got the
answer to some Incredibly Important Question
you never even thought to ask?), raised her
arm, and pointed at me. There was this swirl
of light around her finger . . . for a second I
thought she was gonna go all Zeus on me and
zap me with a bolt of lightning . . . and then—

It appeared out of thin air. I mean, one
minute it wasn't there and the next minute it
was . . . flying across the room on a stream
of purple stardust and landing right in my

hands. I looked down. I couldn't believe it.

"MY DIARY!" I yelled. (Yeah, that's right. I didn't even think to call it a memoir. No way I'm gonna try to put one over on the Fairy Queen.) "I don't understand. How did you . . . ?"

"It's magic, child," Ija said.

"Oh. Right."

"And with magic, the HOW is not important. The WANTING is."

She closed two of her eyes . . . but that third one kept right on looking at me. "You do want it . . . don't you, Kate?"

Did I want it?

Ever since Dr. Faker told my mother I needed to—how'd she put it?—get my "tormented thoughts and feelings" down on paper, I've been pretending that this diary doesn't matter. That I can stop writing in it any time I want and chuck the stupid thing in the incinerator. But right then I realized that I didn't just want the diary . . . I NEEDED it. Needed it more than anything. Whatever was happening to me, I knew that writing about it was the only way I'd ever get through it.

"By the way, Kate," the queen added, almost like it slipped her mind, "I've enchanted it."

"Excuse me?"

"Your diary. I've enchanted it."

I'm thinking What? How? You're kidding? Enchanted! Oh, my GOD!!!!—but you don't want to act like a babbling idiot in front of a queen . . . so I just nodded like it was no big deal and said, "Why, thank you, Your Majesty."

I backed toward the door, so excited I was shaking. For some reason—call it temporary insanity—I tried to curtsy again and this time I really did fall on my butt. And we all laughed. It felt good.

So then we said good-bye again and Martha took me here to my room. (She's staying right across the hall. Gave me this big hug good night and, y'know what? I hugged her right back without batting an eye. Hope I'm not going totally soft.)

Did I say room? It's more like an apartment. Has to be twice the size of our place in Brooklyn—and I don't have to share the bathroom with anyone (considering how long I've been holding it in, that's great news).

There's a humongoid balcony . . . a
four-poster bed . . . paintings of the Landlocked
Warlock, the Sprouting Sorceress, the Burning
Witch and all the rest of the royal family on
the walls (Queen Ija's picture is right over my
bed and that feels great) . . . this amazing
mirror with the most beautiful gold frame I've
ever seen (and this stuff IS real gold. Even I
can tell that) . . . a lamp that goes on and
off just by me thinking it and—

Well, I could go on and on and on about
this, but I am totally wasted. I've been forcing
myself to stay awake for hours now so that
a) I can get all this psycho ranting down on
paper, and b) I can figure out all the insanely
cool things my diary can do now that Ija's put
her magic magumbo in it.

I mean it's wild enough that I'm flipping
through the pages watching my life get turned
into some reality TV show—but there are
things in here that are so personal I never
even wrote about 'em (and, yeah, some of it
IS a little embarrassing, but I guess I can deal
with it—for now at least) and other things I
wasn't even around for—like Old Martha all
alone in her apartment the night she passed
away or the creepy guy with the six arms

(I've got a pretty good idea who THAT is) or—

　　Anyway, I can write more in the morning. Like I said, I'm exhausted . . . and I've gotta conk.

　　I usually have a horrible time falling asleep—but something about being in this place makes me feel the way I did before Herbert the Great left. Before we lost Matty: y'know, all safe and warm. Protected. And loved.

　　I still don't know if there's really such a thing as a "happily ever after"—but, y'know what? I'm willing to give it a shot.

flaring (she was an admirable girl, but hardly perfect), "would say such a thing. This," she continued, stamping her foot, "is Abadazad, and no one here is doomed unless they choose to be."

Master Wix looked around the forbidding cave, then out toward the whirling snows that blew with terrible determination. "I mean no disrespect, Martha, for you know that I adore you." (This was undeniably true.) "And," he continued, "I make no claims to intelligence. In fact, the very act of thinking gives me a miserable headache." (This, too, was undeniable.) "But," he concluded, "given our predicament, I would think that you were the fool, not I."

Little Martha laughed, all temper gone. "Perhaps I am," she said warmly. "The grandest fool who ever lived." She took his hand and guided him toward the mouth of the cave. "But, fool or not, I've learned some things during my adventures here in Queen Ija's kingdom."

"What have you learned?" Master Wix asked.

"I have learned," Little Martha replied, "that the greatest adventures are the ones that seem utterly hopeless. For these," she went on, turning to face him now, "always end in the greatest joy."

"I don't know if I understand that," Wix said, scratching

Good night, Matty.

to be continued . . .

Okay, so I'm gonna show you a little of what happens in the next part of my diary (or journals or memoirs or WHATEVER). I guess if I had to give it a title I'd call it The Dream Thief, since it's mostly about the Lanky Man, but it's also about me, and Matty (of course) and this really bizarro character called Master Wix. It's even weirder than the stuff in the last book . . . but every word of it is true. I SWEAR.

The average idiot on the street would think I'm making this up, but I figure if you're reading this you're NOT an average idiot. You're probably the kind of person who BELIEVES that there's more to this stupid world than the garbage they shove down our throats every night on the six o'clock news. And . . . as Queen Ija once told me . . . when it comes to magic, believing's the MOST IMPORTANT THING.

Kate

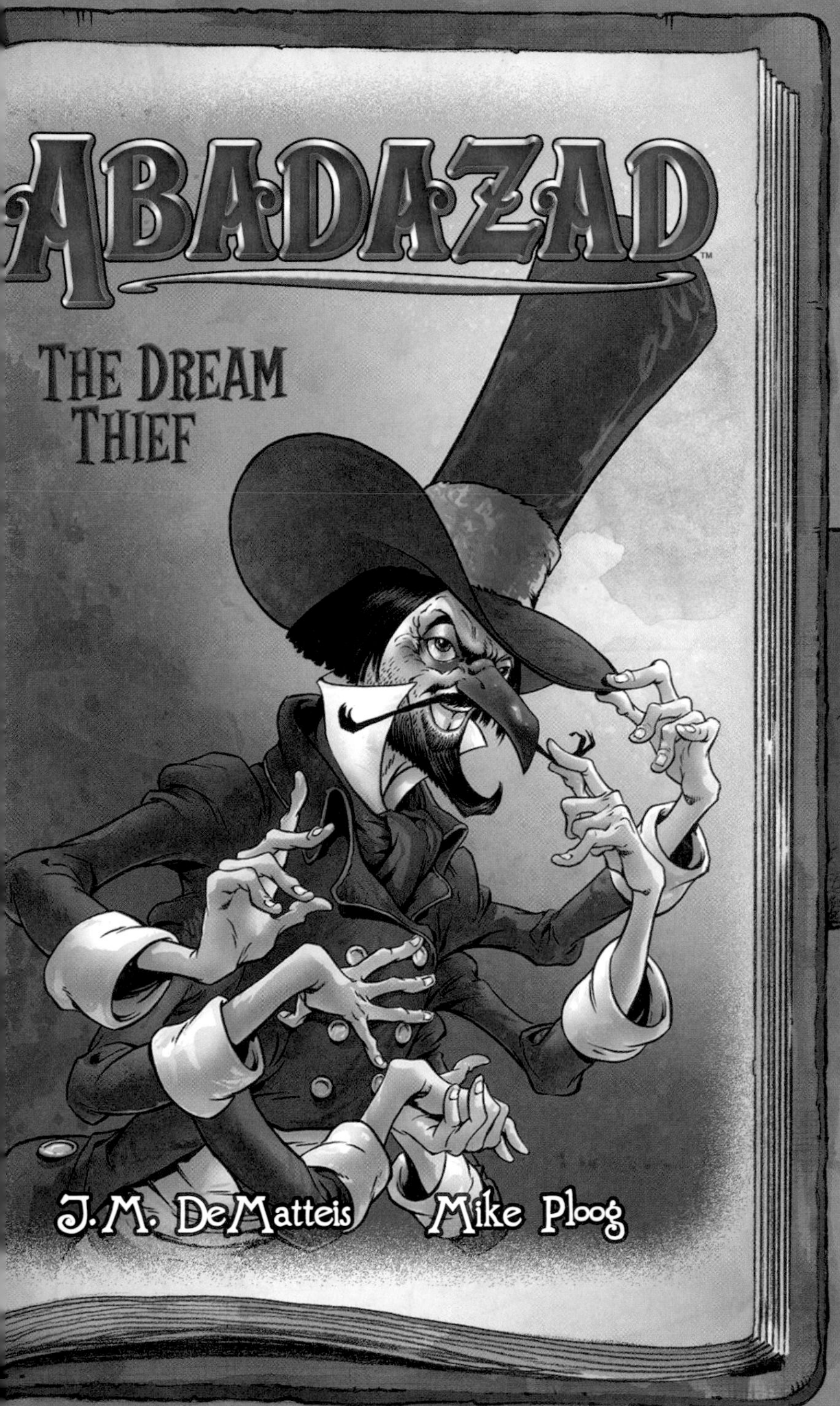
ABADAZAD™
THE DREAM THIEF
J. M. DeMatteis
Mike Ploog

I asked, "Who ARE you, kid?"

He waited a couple of seconds, almost like he was trying to build up the suspense . . . and then his thumb burst into flame. Yeah, you read that right. One instant it was a perfectly normal finger and the next it was all lit up like a Fourth of July sparkler. Then the kid put that burning thumb on the top of his head and SET IT ON FIRE. The whole room was suddenly blazing with light and, pretty quickly, I realized three things:

1) It wasn't his head he lit up, it was some kind of rope, sticking RIGHT OUT OF HIS SCALP. No, not a rope: a wick. A candle wick.

2) The kid (whose clothes, by the way, were even more ridiculous than his shoes—he looked like Buster Brown on a really bad day) was MADE OUT OF WAX. Yeah, you read THAT right, too: wax. Melting and bubbling down the sides of his head.

3) This DEFINITELY wasn't Matty.

Then Wax-Boy flashed me this lopsided grin—more overbite than lip—blew out his thumb, and announced: "Master Wix at your service!"

"Master Wix?" I repeated.

"The one and only!" he exclaimed.

I think I mentioned once that Master Wix was my brother's Absolute Favorite Abadazad Character. Not mine, though: I always thought the kid was kind of pathetic. (Franklin Davies must've felt the same way 'cause he only used Wix in two books . . . which makes him WAY smarter than the morons who made the Abadazad movies. They had Wix as the main character in Abadazad Five. Which explains why there was never an Abadazad SIX.) I mean, here's this kid—who's not a kid, he's an enchanted candle—who spends all his time searching for his parents. Even when people explain to him that he wasn't born, he was MOLDED IN A FACTORY, the dummy keeps right on looking. And believing that he'll find them.

I dunno. Maybe Matty was a lot like Master Wix. Not that HE was dumb. No way. It's just that, after Dad left, Matt never gave up hoping that Herbert the Great would would make some Grand Return. "He'll be back for my birthday," he'd say. Or "I know he'll be home for Christmas." Or Easter. Or Groundhog Day.

Nothing I said—and, believe me, I said plenty—could stop my brother from wishing and hoping. Guess he figured if a lump of wax could act like a living, breathing boy—then why couldn't a lump like Herbert the Great get a sudden burst of the guilts and come running home?

Anyway, Wix trotted over to me, dragging his stuffed animal (which turned out not to be a bear at all but a battered, lumpy dragon). He grabbed my hand in his waxy paw, shook it, and said, "I know I'm supposed t'bow when I meet people—at least that's what Professor Headstrong keeps TELLIN' me—but every time I do I end up splittin' my pants." Then he laughed, kind of like a donkey with asthma. And, I couldn't help it, I laughed, too.

ABADAZAD

THE ROAD TO INCONCEIVABLE

by J.M. DeMatteis

drawings by Mike Ploog

colors by Nick Bell

HYPERION BOOKS FOR CHILDREN
NEW YORK

Printed in the United States of America

First Edition

1 2 3 4 5 6 7 8 9 10

This book is set in CG Whisper

Reinforced binding

ISBN 1-4231-0062-X

Library of Congress Cataloging-in-Publication Data on file

Visit www.hyperionbooksforchildren.com

Managing Editors: Jaime Herbeck, Janet Castiglione
Copy Chief: Monica Mayper
Book Designer: Roberta Pressel
Production Artist: Debbie Lofaso
Production Manager: Nisha Panchal

For my sweet daughter, Katie (the real one!), whose eyes reflect the moons and suns and all the joy that runs through the universe; and, of course, to my oldest and dearest friend, that Master of Master Magicians—Merwan S. Irani

—JMD

To our "Monie" and Route 66

—MP

Gratitude Beyond Words to my wife, Diane, and my son, Cody, for their constant love; and to all the inhabitants of Abadazad for their constant inspiration

—JMD

Thanks to Mark Alessi, Ian Feller and the entire CrossGen crew for believing in magic . . . Michael Farmer for his artistic Third Eye . . . Kevin Cleary and Josh Morris for getting us across the Eight Oceans . . . with a special tip of Queen Ija's crown to Brenda Bowen for her vision and support

—JMD & MP